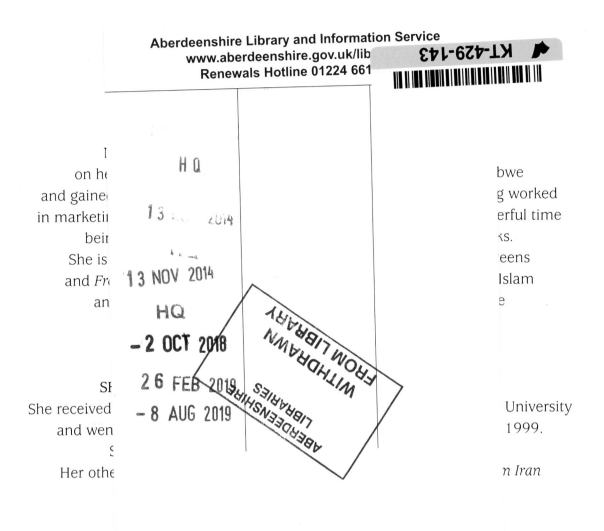

I
on he   bwe
and gaine   g worked
in marketi   erful time
bein   ks.
She is   eens
and *Fr*   Islam
an   e

Sl
She received   University
and wen   1999.
S
Her othe   n *Iran*

Robert, Na'ima B.

For Miriam, Shakira and my moon-gazing sons — *N.R.*

Ramadan Moon copyright © Frances Lincoln Limited 2009
Text copyright © Na'ima B Robert 2009
Illustrations copyright © Shirin Adl 2009
The right of Na'ima B Robert to be identified as the author of this work
and Shirin Adl to be identified as illustrator has been asserted by them
in accordance with the Copyright, Designs and Patents Act,
1988 (United Kingdom).

First published in Great Britain in 2009 and in the USA in 2010 by
Frances Lincoln Children's Books, 4 Torriano Mews,
Torriano Avenue, London NW5 2RZ
www.franceslincoln.com

First paperback edition published in 2011

A catalogue record for this book is available from the British Library.

ISBN 978-1-84780-206-4

Illustrated with watercolour, collage, colour pencils

Set in Usherwood

Printed in Dongguan, Guangdong, China by Toppan Leefung in May 2010

9 8 7 6 5 4 3 2 1

RaMaDaN MOON

Na'ima B Robert

Shirin Adl

F

FRANCES LINCOLN
CHILDREN'S BOOKS

Ramadan, the month of fasting,
Doesn't begin all at once.
It begins with a whisper
And a prayer
And a wish.

As the month of Ramadan approaches,
We search the sky for a sign.
Waiting,
Anticipating,
That silver sliver of brightness,
The shining white crescent
That is the Ramadan Moon.

And when the new moon is seen,
What wonderful excitement!
The news spreads like wildfire
Through cities, towns and villages,
Across deserts and grassland,
Into each and every home.

And Muslims of every nation,
Of every age and every hue
Will join the celebration
Of the arrival of the moon:
"It's here, Ramadan is here,
The Month of Mercy has begun!"

And in mosque after mosque,
Of every shape and size,
Men, women and children
Will all stand up to pray.
The imam will recite the verses
Of the book that was revealed
Hundreds
Upon hundreds
Upon hundreds of years ago.

So now we all wake up to eat,
In the dark before dawn,
Sleepy mouthfuls for the day ahead
While the silent city sleeps.

Then Dad's clear voice rings out,
Calling all of us to pray,
Our family bows, like one body,
Before the break of day.

In daylight, we feel hungry,
But at sunset, when we eat,
It makes us a little thoughtful,
A little humble,
And very grateful.

And each night the moon grows fuller,
Like ripe and tender fruit,
Shining on houses filled with laughter
And mosques alive with prayer.

Each night they come, unfailing,

This seething congregation,

To reflect on the words of their Lord

In silent celebration.

During the day we keep busy
With all sorts of good deeds:
Our voices flow with the words of God
In unplanned harmonies.
We look for things to give away,
Collect money for charity,
Be kind and caring and polite,
Try hard not to get angry.

Now the Ramadan moon is round and full,

A bright silver medallion,

But with a special, secret sorrow,

We see that half the month is gone.

We watch her as she wanes,

Losing a sliver every night

Until we reach the last ten days,

Those last days tinged with sadness,

When we try to share more,

Pray more,

Do more,

And give more.

And we look for the Night of Power,
Better than a thousand nights.
That extra-special night
When we ask for all that we desire,
Wishes upon wishes
And prayer upon prayer.

But then the last ten days become the last five,

The last four nights become the last three,

The last two,

The last . . .

And when the new crescent moon is seen
And the Eid day is announced,
The Muslim world rejoices
For our festival has begun.

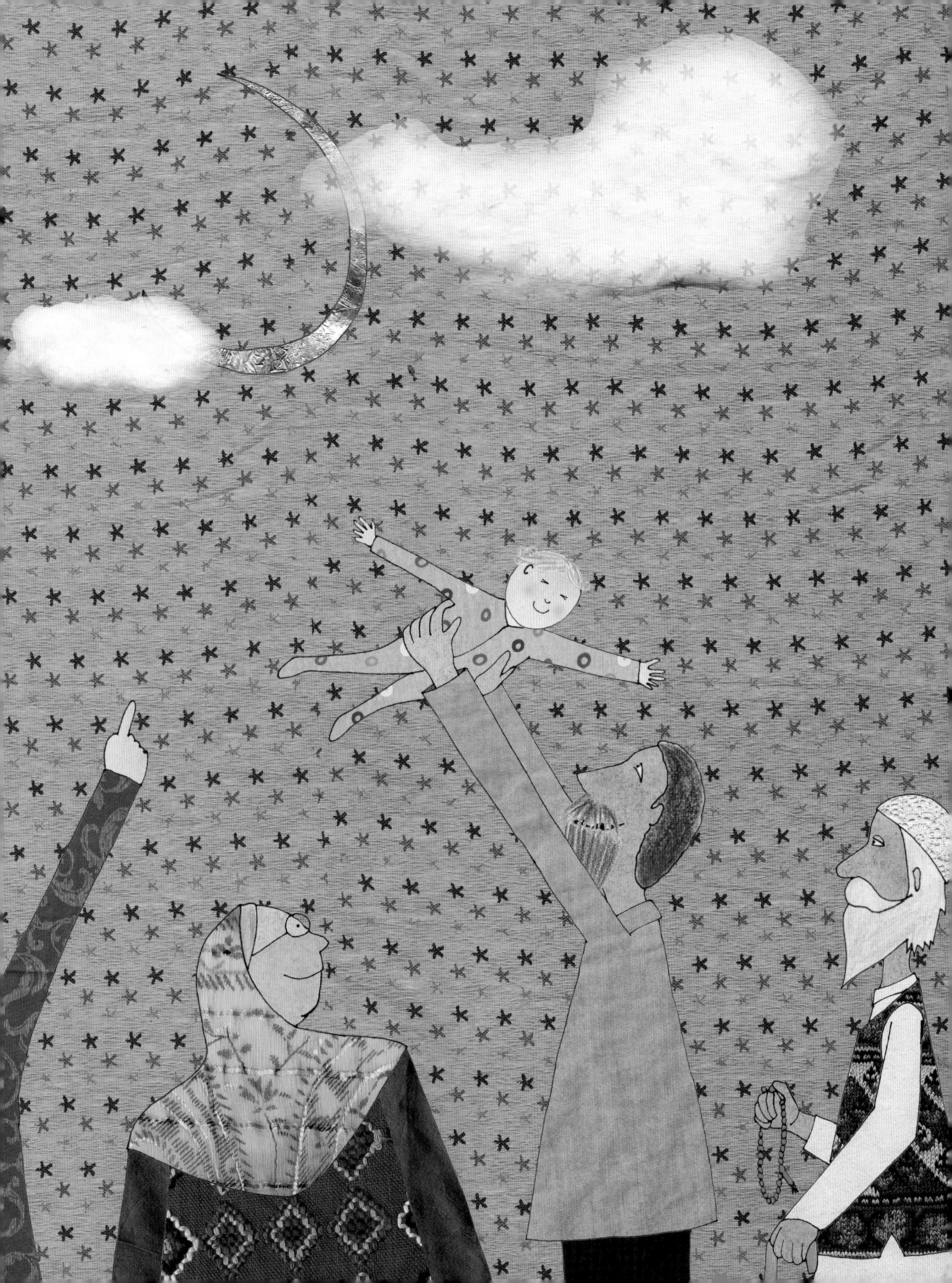

For Eid there will be haircuts

And pretty henna patterns

And visitors

And brand new clothes that rustle as we walk.

And in the morning
There will be the Eid prayer,
Charity for the poor,
Family and friends,
Parties and outings,
Sweets and treats and more . . .

But all that is tomorrow.

Tonight the city sleeps.

As I look out at the night sky,

My smile is bittersweet.

Goodbye, great Month of Mercy,

Hope to see you soon.

Please hurry back, my silver friend,

My beautiful Ramadan Moon.